THE LURKER'S LAW

THE SYSTEM IS BROKEN. HE ISN'T

PRATIK MISHRA

The Lurker's Law uses a dark, gritty, and suspense-driven tone, combining psychological realism with crime thriller conventions. The language is sharp, precise, and haunting, reflecting both the internal turmoil of the killer and the decaying moral fabric of society. Graphic depictions of violence are intentional and serve to underline the brutality of both the crimes committed and the justice delivered. This story challenges conventional perspectives, and readers are urged to engage with it not as a justification of violence, but as an exploration of morality, justice, and trauma.

Contents

Foreword

Some stories are born in light. Others crawl out of the dark. The Lurker's Law belongs to the latter.

This is not your typical crime thriller. This is a psychological excavation, a tale that burrows deep into the dirt of justice denied.

In the shadows of society, there are criminals wearing masks of innocence, and innocents suffering in silence.

And then there are shadows darker still, the ones who decide to fix what the law refuses to.

This book introduces you to a killer who does not kill for sport or money. He kills only those who once destroyed others.

It is not a book for the faint of heart. But it is one for those who dare to ask:

"When evil goes unpunished, who dares to punish evil?"

Preface

The seed for The Lurker's Law was born out of a question we all ask but rarely answer:
"What if justice isn't served?"
This story isn't about glorifying a killer. It's about exploring the shadow of every broken verdict, every survivor unheard, every criminal freed by loopholes.
The Lurker is not a hero, nor is he a monster in the traditional sense. He is what society created when it turned its back.
I wanted to create a psychological portrait of a man who feels, deeply, and kills, mercilessly. A man whose mind is a warzone between vengeance and virtue.
As you read, you will question right and wrong, law and loophole, good and evil.
And maybe, just maybe, you'll wonder who The Lurker is in your world.

Acknowledgements

I owe immense gratitude to the minds and hearts that supported this work in silence and strength.

To my creative community, thank you for believing in this story even when it walked the razor's edge of morality.

To every late-night discussion, every critique, and every shared shiver, your insights made this more than a story.

A special thanks to those who understand the weight of justice when justice remains blind.

And lastly, to the ones who inspired the victims and the vigilante, you know who you are.

This book is for you.

— Pratik Mishra

Prologue

The sound of a leaking tap echoed in the silence, each drop hitting the rusted basin like a metronome counting down to something unspeakable.

He stood barefoot in the center of the room—concrete beneath, shadows above, and blood smeared across the linoleum wall like a forgotten mural of pain. His breathing was calm. Too calm.

A body lay behind him. Tied. Gagged. Still twitching.

Not from life—but from the body's refusal to accept it had lost.

In his gloved hand, he held a voice recorder—old, scratched, and labeled in black ink: "Confessions."

"You molested four girls. The youngest was seven. And the court gave you two years. But you served six months. You smiled outside that gate. Do you remember that smile?"

The man on the floor whimpered. Tears rolled down his cheeks. Not from guilt. From fear.

"You don't deserve a trial. You had one. Society failed. Now it's my turn."

Click.

The knife was small. Surgical. Clean.

By the time the sun rose, the world would have one less predator. And no one would know who did it.

No fingerprints. No cameras. No witnesses.

Just a body. A symbol.

A whisper.

The press would call it the work of a vigilante. The public would debate. The police would stumble in the dark. And somewhere deep in the alleys of the city, the Lurker would vanish again—until another name crossed his path.

Because this was no longer revenge.

It was doctrine.

The Lurker's Law had just begun.

First Kill

The city was dark, not the darkness that a blackout brings, but a suffocating kind that wrapped itself around every corner, leaving the streets eerily deserted. The flickering streetlights cast long shadows on the pavement, and the cool breeze whispered through the empty alleyways. It was the night that made people uneasy, like something was about to happen, but they couldn't put their finger on what.

A young man, no older than 28, rushed down the street. His name was Alex Porter, and to the outside world, he seemed like just another face in the crowd. He had a normal life at work, friends, and responsibilities. But deep within, he carried a weight that no one could see. The knowledge of the system's failings and frequent injustices weighed heavily on him. His mind wandered back to the horrors he'd witnessed, the unspeakable acts that people like him were helpless to stop.

He turned a corner and stopped in front of an abandoned building. His breath caught for a moment, a slight hesitation in his step. The structure was old, its windows boarded up, the metal door hanging off its hinges. It is a perfect hideout for someone trying to escape their past or their future.

Inside, a single figure moved with practiced ease, shifting through the shadows. The Lurker had arrived. And this was his first kill.

The target was a man named Gregory Carter. A businessman by day, but a monster by night. Known for his connections with the underground criminal world, Carter had eluded the authorities for years. Heavily invested in the system, he had been a part of it, using his wealth and power to manipulate the law for his benefit. He was the type of person who believed that money could fix anything, including the atrocities he committed. He was a rapist, a murderer, his crimes were many, but his punishment had never arrived.

Alex stood in the shadow, watching. His heart raced as the Lurker approached, his steps silent against the cold concrete. He had been tracking Carter for weeks, watching his every move, studying his patterns. It was almost time.

The Lurker's hands were steady, his gaze unwavering. He moved like a shadow, blending into the darkness, his presence barely noticed by anyone, even those closest to him. Carter's time had come.

The man entered the building, his heavy boots echoing against the walls. He was unaware of the danger lurking in the shadows, oblivious to the judgment that was about to be passed on him.

Alex felt a strange calmness come over him as he heard the door creak open. He knew what was going to happen. He had planned this moment. Having studied, he knew the way of the Lurker. He knew exactly what to expect.

There was a brief struggle. Carter yelled in a low, gruff voice. He tried to fight back, but it was no use. The Lurker had him in his grip. There was a sharp, desperate scream.

Alex didn't need to look. He already knew how this would end. The Lurker was methodical was no random act of violence; it was justice.

Minutes later, the sound of silence filled the room. The Lurker stood, his figure partially illuminated by the faint moonlight coming through the broken window. Blood stained his clothes, but his eyes showed no remorse. He had done what needed to be done,

Alex stepped forward from the shadows, his heart pounding. He had watched the entire thing unfold, the raw power of the Lurker in action. He couldn't help but feel a mix of awe and fear. This man, this shadow of justice, was doing what Alex and the police could not. He was cleaning up the streets, one criminal at a time.

But something gnawed at the back of Alex's mind. Something he couldn't shake. Was this truly justice? Or was it just another form of revenge?

The Lurker turned, his eyes meeting Alex's. There was no fear in his gaze, only understanding.

"It's done," the Lurker said, his voice cold, as if he were speaking to no one in particular.

Alex nodded, swallowing hard. The weight of what had just happened was heavy on his chest. He didn't know whether he should feel relieved or terrified. All he knew was that the Lurker had taken the first step in a war, one that Alex might not stop.

CHAPTER II

The Method Behind the Madness

The city had long since grown accustomed to the absence of justice for certain crimes. Murders, rapes, and assaults were all common under the veil of anonymity and indifference. Criminals lived comfortably in the shadows, untouched by law enforcement, insulated by their wealth, power, or sheer luck. But as with all things, the cycle of disorder must inevitably meet the backlash of consequence.

In the deepest recesses of a crumbling apartment complex, beneath the hum of neon lights and the scent of stale air, the Lurker sat. His eyes, dark pools of unspoken thoughts, crawled over the image before him. The picture was of his second victim, a well-known figure in the criminal underworld. Marcus Hawke, a notorious drug lord who had, for years, evaded the law, had been untouchable. Now, the Lurker was preparing to make him accountable.

But the method was not one of blind rage. No, the Lurker had a plan. He always did.

The Lurker's weapon of choice was not a gun, nor was it a knife. His hands were tools of precision, his mind a machine designed to calibrate every detail, to ensure that the justice he sought to deliver was untraceable, immaculate. The killings were never spontaneous. They were an art, a morbid art, but art nonetheless. Every murder had a story, every method, a carefully crafted purpose. There was no room for chaos or emotion to cloud the process.

It began with research.

The Lurker did not simply strike in the dead of night without knowing every facet of his target's life. He studied them. His first victim, a man named Philip Gregory, a white-collar criminal, had spent weeks under the Lurker's scrutiny. His social media was cataloged, and his routines were tracked. The Lurker even sat across the street from his house on numerous occasions, noting his comings and goings. The same process applied to every victim since.

He knew what they would do, how they would react, what weaknesses they harbored. He was not just seeking revenge; he was seeking to deliver justice with the most meticulous of designs. His first kill had been a failure in his eyes. The execution had been messy, the crime scene far too public. He had been sloppy, and that was not a mistake the Lurker would allow again.

The planning stages for Marcus Hawke's death were now in full swing. The Lurker had learned every detail about Hawke, how he moved, where he lived, what time he spent in his luxurious penthouse, and when he took his evening walks along the river. It was during one of these walks that the Lurker would strike. But not in the way anyone would expect.

Marcus was a man of routine. Every evening, around 9 PM, he would walk alone for exactly 30 minutes. He was a man who believed in his own invincibility, often without protection, and without fear of being attacked. The Lurker would use this weakness against him.

The plan was simple, yet intricate. The Lurker had already secured a route—one that would take Hawke past an abandoned building, which the Lurker had turned into a trap.

A few days earlier...

The Lurker stood in the shadows of the derelict building, a quiet figure beneath the harsh lights of a distant streetlamp. His breath was shallow, his fingers twitching with anticipation. He had been here for days, working to set up the scene. This was his masterpiece.

He had removed the building's broken windows and set up a series of tripwires within. Once Marcus entered the building, the wire would trigger a minor explosion, sending pieces of debris across the ground in a controlled burst. The explosion itself wasn't the goal; it was the chaos it would create. The moment Marcus would be startled, that was when the Lurker would make his move.

The plan was flawless.

As Marcus stepped onto the deserted pathway, his footsteps echoed against the pavement. The Lurker's mind focused on the beat of each step, calculating the distance, timing everything to perfection. From his hidden position, the Lurker watched the man with detached interest.

The sense of power he felt from controlling this moment was intoxicating. He wasn't just killing for revenge; he was fixing something deeply broken within the fabric of society. Hawke, like many others before him, had escaped punishment for his crimes, and now the Lurker would be the instrument of justice. His grip tightened around the wire, the signal to set the plan in motion.

Marcus walked closer.

The explosion went off with a sharp crack. It wasn't enough to cause significant harm, but it was enough to disorient him. Marcus staggered backward, hands up to shield his face from the dust and flying debris.

At that very moment, the Lurker emerged from the darkness. His movements were like a predator's silent, calculated, and swift. Before Marcus could even react, a long blade gleamed under the pale light of the moon, cutting through the air with deadly precision.

CHAPTER III

Alice's Obsession

Alice didn't ask questions. Not in the way people were supposed to, at least. She wasn't like the others who came in and out of the police station with their mundane lives. Alice's presence always lingered, her eyes sharp, almost calculating, as if she could see things no one else could. The detectives didn't understand her, and frankly, they were unnerved by her calm demeanor. But Alice wasn't here for them; she wasn't even here for the case.

She was here for him.

It had been two months since the first murder, and already the name "The Lurker" had made its way through every criminal gossip network. Everyone knew someone who knew someone who was connected to a victim. The police, however, had no idea. They didn't understand what was happening or why the murders seemed to target only the worst offenders in the city. No one could connect the dots except Alice.

Alice wasn't a detective. She wasn't a journalist either. Alice wasn't anything that anyone would consider being special, at least on the surface. She was a server at a dive bar in the seedy part of the city. No one paid her much attention. That was until she started to notice things small things. A glance here, a phrase whispered there, an odd movement in the shadows. She always had her ear to the ground, always listening, always watching. And when she heard the whispers about The Lurker, something clicked in her.

The name haunted her and drew her in like a moth to a flame. She could feel the darkness in him, something that spoke to the anger she'd buried deep inside herself. A part of her admired what he was doing. He was punishing those who deserved it. The kind of people who walked free every day without a care for their actions, hiding behind their money, power, and connections. But another part of her wondered if she could ever understand the madness that drove him.

And so she became obsessed.

It started subtly. She would stay up late at night, tracking the news stories, reading the case files, and looking for any connection between the victims. She knew she was doing something dangerous, but the thrill of it, the pull, was too powerful. Every crime scene picture she saw only fueled her fascination further. The way The Lurker operated so methodically, so cleanly, made her blood run cold and, yet, alive.

But it wasn't just the kills that drew her in. It was the pattern. She saw it. She could see the logic behind the madness.

Alice sat at her small kitchen table, the dim light above casting long shadows across the room. The map in front of her was littered with photographs of the victims, all pinned to various points on the map like a puzzle. She ran her finger along the lines, tracing a path that only she seemed to understand.

The Lurker didn't just kill at random. Each victim had a connection to the next, a trail that was slowly forming. She'd seen this before, in the dark corners of criminal psychology, the concept of a ritual, a need for order in the chaos.

"Why did he kill them?" Alice muttered to herself, her voice barely a whisper.

As she sat, her mind drifted to her past. Alice wasn't a stranger to darkness. She had her share of tragedy her father had been a violent man, a criminal himself, and her mother had been too weak to stop it. Growing up in that environment had shaped Alice into something else something cold, something calculating. She had learned the art of survival at a young age, and she knew how to manipulate people without them even realizing it.

But it wasn't until she met The Lurker's victims that the genuine horror started to take shape in her mind. There was something cathartic in his actions, a sense of retribution that echoed her desire for justice. She understood, maybe even more than she was willing to admit, what drove him.

And that's when she began to notice the patterns in her own life, the things that connected her to the killer. It was as though he was reaching out, his every move speaking to something deep within her. Something that had been hidden for years. She began to feel like they were connected, that The Lurker wasn't just some stranger out there in the world, but someone she knew... or could know.

The obsession deepened with each passing day. Alice started to take risks, putting herself in places she never should have been, trying to learn more about the killer. She would overhear conversations at bars, slip into criminal circles, listening for any whispers of The Lurker. She was careful, always playing the part of the innocent bystander. But deep down, she was no longer just a spectator. She was part of the game now.

She needed to see him, needed to understand the man behind the mask.

It was during one of these late-night ventures, after a long shift at the bar, when Alice finally came across the name she'd been searching for—Oliver Bennett. A name that had appeared in the police reports, but with no actual information attached to it. The Lurker's real name was out there, buried beneath layers of speculation and false leads. But Alice found it.

With trembling hands, she pulled out her phone and typed in the name. She found an old news article, one from years ago, when Oliver Bennett had been a minor player in a string of arson cases. The article mentioned him briefly—just enough to get a hint of his background. It was a start, but Alice needed more.

She could feel the electricity in the air as she tried to connect the dots. Oliver Bennett was just another forgotten name in a city that had long since stopped caring about justice. But Alice wasn't done yet. She could feel the tension tightening around her, the invisible string pulling her deeper into the mystery.

It was late when Alice finally put the pieces together. She had spent hours combing through records, notes, and even photographs. She'd built a profile—a portrait of a man who was more than just a killer. He was someone who had seen the worst the world had to offer and chose to become something worse in return.

But it wasn't just about him. It was about her now. She had become obsessed, consumed by the search for a man who could have been a mirror of her soul. The darkness inside her had been awakened, and there was no going back.

CHAPTER IV

The Mind of the Lurker

The night was silent, heavy with the kind of quiet that only comes after something terrible has happened. The Lurker's latest victim had been left at the edge of a run-down alley, discarded like trash, but the brutality of the murder was anything but forgotten. The police were scrambling, trying to make sense of the grisly scene, but no one knew what to make of it. No one, except for Alice.

Alice stood at the edge of the police tape, her eyes locked on the body, analyzing every detail with the precision of a surgeon. The bloodstains on the ground, the broken limbs, the suffocating smell of decay, it all fit into the same twisted narrative that had started weeks ago.

But tonight, something was different. This wasn't just another random victim in the Lurker's path. No, this time, Alice could feel it in her gut. There was a deeper meaning here. A message.

She closed her eyes for a moment, and in the darkness behind her eyelids, she imagined herself stepping into the Lurker's shoes. What was he thinking as he committed these murders? Was it an act of rage? Was it a calculated strike against the criminals of the city, or was it something more?

The Lurker's mind was a labyrinth. No one could truly understand him, not unless they had walked the same path, seen the same horrors. His victims weren't random; they were carefully chosen. He was an architect of chaos, sculpting his vision of justice. But Alice wasn't afraid of him. Not anymore. She was drawn to him, fascinated by the way his mind worked. She knew that understanding him meant understanding herself.

The Lurker's first kill had been an impulsive one, born from the overwhelming rage of watching a criminal walk free, escaping the law. But over time, something had shifted. The killings became more precise, more ritualistic. He had grown colder, more detached. It wasn't just about avenging the wronged anymore. It had become a game a pursuit of something greater than himself.

He had learned how to hide in plain sight, becoming a ghost. No one knew who he was, not even Alice, despite her obsession. His identity was wrapped in layers of misdirection, false trails, and deliberate distractions. Yet, she could feel him getting closer. She could hear his footsteps in the distance, a shadow stalking the edge of her consciousness.

Days passed. Weeks, even. But Alice wasn't letting go of her pursuit. Every lead, every clue, every new piece of information she discovered about The Lurker only made her more obsessed. And then, one evening, after hours of scouring old police reports, she found something that made her heart race.

A pattern.

The first victim had been a man with a history of sexual assault, a man who had used his wealth and influence to escape justice time and time again. The second had been a murderer, a man who had killed his own family in cold blood. The third had been a corrupt cop, someone who had used his badge to intimidate and destroy the lives of innocent people. Each death had been justified in the eyes of the killer. The Lurker wasn't just killing criminals; he was killing people who had slipped through the cracks of the law. People who deserved to die, in his mind.

But as Alice pieced the pattern together, she realized something chilling. Each victim had been a person with a dark history someone whose crime had gone unnoticed, buried beneath lies and wealth. But there was more. She had seen it in the eyes of the dead: a story told through the eyes of the victim, an unspeakable truth hidden in the details.

Alice found herself at a crossroads. She could follow the clues to their inevitable conclusion, or she could back away. But that wasn't in her nature. She wasn't about to walk away from the greatest story she'd ever uncovered. She had to get closer to The Lurker. She had to understand what made him tick.

She began to study his methods more closely, examining the scenes of his crimes with a psychological lens. She wondered if there was something she could learn from him, some kind of truth that she could apply to her own life. Every detail of his crimes screamed to her a desperate cry for justice, a plea to fix what had been broken in the world.

But what did that mean for Alice? Was she becoming like him? Was she willing to cross that line?

Late one night, after yet another uneventful shift at the bar, Alice was sitting alone in her apartment, surrounded by her notebooks and maps. She felt a strange calm wash over her. It was as though everything had been leading her here, to this very moment. She picked up her phone and dialed a number she had kept hidden for weeks.

A voice on the other end answered quickly. "You're still following him, aren't you?"

"Yes," Alice whispered, her breath catching in her throat. "I'm close. I can feel it. I know what he's doing."

The voice laughed softly. "You have no idea, do you?"

It was then that Alice realized the chilling truth: she wasn't alone in this pursuit. Someone else had been watching, too. Someone who knew more than they were letting on. Someone who might even be closer to The Lurker than Alice could have ever imagined.

CHAPTER V

The Hunter Becomes the Hunted

The darkness of the city had always concealed secrets, secrets so deep that even the faintest glimmers of light failed to pierce through. In this darkness, The Lurker had thrived. He had killed without remorse, executed his justice with precision, and disappeared like a whisper in the wind. But tonight, something was different. Tonight, The Lurker wasn't the hunter. Tonight, he was being hunted.

It had been days since his last kill. The city was quieter now, its streets filled with an eerie calm. The Lurker's mind had always thrived in such silence this sense of peace, broken only by his thoughts and the occasional rustling of wind through trees. But a sharp, nagging sensation in the pit of his stomach shattered that stillness. He had felt it before, a sense that someone was watching him.

He had never been afraid. Fear was a weakness, a flaw that criminals in his city had lived with for far too long. But this was different. There was a presence, something he couldn't explain, something that had his mind racing in ways it had never done before. It was a sense of being out of control something he had always managed to avoid until now.

The Lurker's hideout was a small, abandoned building in the industrial district. The walls, once white, were now grey with age and neglect. The windows were boarded up, and the door was reinforced with metal. It had been his sanctuary for months, the one place where he felt safe. But now, it felt like a trap.

He had no reason to think that anyone could track him here. The Lurker was meticulous. He knew how to cover his tracks and erase his presence like a shadow that was never there. But as he sat in his darkened room, staring at the monitor screens that displayed various corners of the city, something gnawed at him. It wasn't the usual feeling of triumph after his kills. It was a feeling of unease.

The air in the room grew thick with tension. He glanced at the clock 2:00 AM. The city was asleep, but his instincts told him that wasn't the case. He could feel eyes on him. He couldn't explain it, but he knew he was being watched.

"No one knows where I am," he whispered to himself, trying to reassure his mind. But the words felt hollow, as though the universe itself was mocking him. He leaned forward, studying the monitors more intently. The streets, the alleyways, the abandoned buildings everything seemed normal. Too normal. But that's when he saw it.

A figure is barely visible in the corner of one of the security cameras. It wasn't a man he recognized. It wasn't a shadow he could explain. The figure was too still, too deliberate in its movements. It was watching his hideout.

Alice had been following The Lurker for weeks. At first, it was just a hunch a strange feeling that the missing criminals were connected to something larger. But the more she investigated, the more she discovered. The pattern was undeniable. Every time someone disappeared, it was as though the city itself was holding its breath.

Alice had worked as a detective for years. She was no stranger to cases that seemed impossible, unsolvable, or downright dangerous. But this case... this was different. She had always prided herself on being able to piece together puzzles, to catch the criminals who thought they were untouchable. But The Lurker... The Lurker was a puzzle that had no solution.

She had spent sleepless nights poring over reports, photos, and crime scene photos, trying to connect the dots. Every piece pointed back to one thing: The Lurker. He was the one who had been taking justice into his own hands. And now it was time to stop him.

The Lurker felt the weight of the moment pressing down on him. For the first time in months, he wasn't sure how to proceed. He had been so careful, so deliberate in his actions, but now he was being stalked. And it was a feeling that made his blood run cold.

He needed to act fast. The element of surprise was his greatest weapon, but it wouldn't matter if someone had already figured him out. He couldn't afford to let anyone, especially Alice, get too close. She was too smart, too persistent. And that meant that he had to eliminate the threat before it became a problem.

He grabbed his coat from the hook by the door and slipped it on, pulling his mask over his face. His weapons were already hidden in the pockets of his jacket everything he needed to disappear without a trace. The Lurker didn't leave things to chance. He was prepared for everything.

He took one last look at the monitors. The figure outside was still there, standing motionless under the dim glow of the streetlight. It was almost as though the world itself had frozen in time, waiting for the inevitable confrontation.

Alice's heart pounded in her chest as she observed The Lurker's hideout through the scope of her rifle. She had been tracking him for days, and tonight was supposed to be the end of the chase. Her team had set up surveillance in the area, and she knew that it was only a matter of time before he made his move. She was ready for it.

Alice wasn't just a detective. She had spent years training for this moment. She knew how to anticipate her enemy's next move, how to think like them, how to be two steps ahead. But there was something different from The Lurker. Something that made him unpredictable. Something that made him dangerous.

She adjusted the focus on her rifle's scope, her eyes narrowing as she saw movement in the distance. The Lurker was leaving his hideout.

Her pulse quickened. This was the moment she had been waiting for. The trap had been set. All she had to do was pull the trigger.

But something stopped her. A voice in her head, a warning, telling her to be careful. The Lurker was dangerous, yes, but he was also smart. He would know they were watching him.

As The Lurker stepped out of the building and into the street, he felt the eyes on him again. He didn't know who was watching or where they were, but he knew he wasn't alone anymore. He was being hunted.

His mind raced as he walked toward the alley, each step calculated, every move

Deliberate. He knew that the time for hiding was over. The time for killing was coming. And tonight, it would be his greatest hunt yet.

The Lurker was not just a killer. He was a man driven by a sense of justice, albeit his twisted version of it. But tonight, as the hunter and the hunted became blurred, something inside him shifted. He wasn't sure what it was fear, adrenaline, or something else entirely, but he knew that the game had changed.

For the first time, he wasn't just trying to escape his past. He was running from a future that had already caught up with him.

The Lurker disappears into the shadows of the city, pursued by an unseen force Alice who is determined to put an end to his reign of terror.

CHAPTER VI

The Lurker's Strategy

The night had grown colder, the city's skyline shrouded in a haze of pollution and smoke. The Lurker knew the streets well, but tonight, the city seemed unfamiliar. Every alley, every streetlight, every echo of footsteps felt like it belonged to someone else. A singular thought consumed his mind; He was being watched.

The Lurker paused at the edge of the alley, his senses heightened. He could feel the weight of the silence, the unnatural stillness that surrounded him. It was as if the city itself had held its breath, waiting for something to happen. The sound of distant sirens echoed in the background, but it did little to mask the growing sense of unease in the air.

He had planned his movements carefully: every escape route, every exit his entire life had been a game of strategy. But tonight, the strategy felt different. It wasn't about him hunting criminals. Tonight, the rules had shifted. He was no longer in control.

His fingers drummed lightly on the edge of the cold brick wall, a nervous tick he had never noticed before. He couldn't let his guard down. Not now. Not with Alice so close on his heels.

Alice had been watching him for hours. The night was long, the tension between them palpable. She had never been this close to her target. The Lurker had always managed to stay one step ahead of the law, but Alice was different. She wasn't just a cop. She was a predator in her own right. She had learned from the best, and her instincts told her that tonight, she had a chance to end this chase.

She leaned back in her position, her rifle still in her grip. The streetlights flickered above, casting long shadows across the empty street. She knew he would come out soon. He always did. The Lurker wasn't someone who hid indefinitely. He always had a plan. And so did she.

The Lurker's mind raced as he continued walking down the alley. He couldn't shake the feeling that Alice was close, but he wasn't sure where she was. He knew she was good. Too good. That's why he had to be smarter, faster, more unpredictable. Alice had the patience to wait for hours, even days, to catch him. But tonight, she would find out that the tables had turned.

He ducked into a narrow passageway, hidden from view, and quickly made his way to a nearby rooftop. From here, he could see the entire street below, every move, every shadow. His advantage was the city itself, its labyrinth of buildings, rooftops, and alleyways. He knew these streets better than anyone, and it was in the shadows that he thrived.

Alice's eyes narrowed as she adjusted the focus on her scope. She had seen him disappear into the alley, but she hadn't expected him to vanish so quickly. She had anticipated him using the rooftops, it was one of the few places in the city where he could move undetected. She wasn't foolish. She knew his tricks.

She had been preparing for this moment. She had set up traps, studied his patterns, and anticipated his every move. She had been tracking The Lurker for weeks, and she had pieced together a strategy of her own.

Alice wasn't going to let him slip away this time.

The Lurker watched from the rooftop, his sharp eyes scanning the street below. He could feel Alice's presence like a weight on his chest. He wasn't sure how much time he had before she realized where he was, but he wasn't going to wait around to find out.

He reached into his jacket pocket and pulled out a small device. It was a simple gadget, nothing fancy, but it was enough. With a click, the device emitted a small but powerful signal that scrambled the frequencies in the area. It would disrupt any surveillance equipment nearby, including Alice's rifle scope and the cameras on the street.

The city was his playing field, and tonight, he was going to take full advantage of it.

Alice's rifle scope flickered for a moment. She frowned, adjusting the lens to compensate for the interference. Her instincts told her that something was wrong. The signal wasn't just a random glitch it was deliberate. The Lurker was actively jamming the frequencies. It was a tactic she had seen before, but never this precisely.

She exhaled sharply, her grip tightening on the rifle. This wasn't just a game anymore. The Lurker was testing her, seeing how far she would go. But Alice had already made her decision. She wasn't backing down.

The Lurker's lips curled into a smirk. He could almost feel the frustration radiating off Alice from up here. The longer he stayed hidden, the more desperate she would become. It was part of his plan. He wanted her to make a mistake. He wanted her to feel the pressure. And when she did, he would strike.

But as he stood there, looking down at the city, something inside him shifted. He had been so focused on escaping Alice's pursuit that he hadn't stopped to think about what this had all become.

This wasn't just about crime or justice. This was about him. About his own need to prove something to himself, to the city, to Alice.

And he was getting tired.

Alice made the decision. She knew it wasn't going to be easy, but she had to act now. The Lurker wasn't just a criminal. He was a symbol of everything that was wrong with this city. And she wasn't going to let him get away.

She slipped out of her hiding place, moving silently through the shadows. She had spent years training for moments like this—silent, calculated, and deadly. She knew that time was running out, and if she didn't act soon, she would lose her only chance to catch The Lurker.

The Lurker turned away from the rooftop ledge, his mind racing. He had spent so long running from the law, from people like Alice, but tonight, he was facing something new. He was facing himself. The Lurker was tired of being a ghost in the shadows. He was tired of running.

He had spent his life creating chaos, punishing the guilty, and hiding in the dark. But now, in the stillness of the night, he wondered if it was all worth it. What had he accomplished?

The Lurker had built an empire of fear, but it was a house made of sand. And tonight, as Alice closed in on him, he realized just how fragile that empire was.

Alice closed the distance between them, her breathing steady. She had anticipated every move The Lurker could make. But what she hadn't expected was his hesitation. She had seen it in his eyes when he turned away from the rooftop ledge.

This was it.

The Lurker's gaze shifted toward the shadows of the alley. For the first time, he wasn't sure if he could escape. Alice was too close, and the city felt too small. His heart pounded in his chest as the realization hit him; tonight might be the night that the hunter became the hunted.

The Lurker finally realizes the consequences of his actions and the escalating pursuit by Alice, who is determined to end his reign.

25

CHAPTER VII

A Descent into Madness

The streets were deserted now. A thick fog rolled in from the bay, swallowing the city whole. Every corner seemed unfamiliar, every shadow a potential threat. The Lurker felt the walls closing in on him as he moved through the misty alleys. His heartbeat quickened with each step he took, and he couldn't shake the feeling that he was being hunted though for once, it wasn't just Alice on his tail. No, it was something darker. Something deeper.

His mind had started to fracture. What had once been a sharp, calculated focus was now slipping, unraveling like a loose thread. He couldn't trust his thoughts anymore. Each passing day, each kill, each near-miss had twisted something inside him. His motivations had changed. Where once there was clarity, now there was nothing but a growing emptiness.

The Lurker wasn't just a predator anymore. He had become the very thing he once loathed. His actions, once driven by a sense of justice, had blurred into something far more sinister. He wasn't just punishing criminals he was indulging in it. The thrill of the hunt had become an addiction, and he found himself craving it more and more.

Alice, on the other hand, was beginning to understand the monster she was chasing. She had spent months studying The Lurker, learning his every move, his every strategy. But nothing could prepare her for the psychological depths of his descent. She had seen him as a criminal, yes but now she was beginning to see something much worse. He wasn't just a man with a mission. He was a man who had lost his humanity.

Alice had always prided herself on her ability to control her emotions, but as the chase continued, she felt herself slipping. The adrenaline had become her constant companion, and every time she closed in on The Lurker, it felt like she was one step closer to losing herself.

She knew that the moment she captured him, the game would be over. But part of her feared what might happen to her once the chase ended. What if she, too, became obsessed? What if this relentless pursuit had already started to erode her sense of self?

The Lurker reached the edge of the city, his feet crunching the dry leaves as he stepped into the woods. The air here was different, heavier, filled with a quiet that made his ears ring. The fog had thickened, and the city's noises were now distant, faint echoes lost in the vastness of the wilderness.

He stopped and looked back, his eyes narrowing as he listened for any sign of pursuit. The Lurker was no longer sure whether Alice was still following him or whether his paranoia was making him hear things. His fingers twitched, itching for the rush of the hunt. He wanted the thrill, but tonight, it felt different.

Alice was at the edge of the city too, but unlike The Lurker, she wasn't running. She was waiting. She had tracked him through the fog, every footstep a reminder of how close she was. She knew the moment would come when they would face each other, and she was prepared. Despite that, her heart raced.

Her mind kept replaying their previous encounters, each one more desperate than the last. She had begun to feel like the chase wasn't just about catching him anymore. It had become personal.

She had learned too much about him, perhaps more than she ever should have. And now, as the city faded behind her, Alice couldn't help but wonder what would happen once it was all over. Would she be able to walk away, untouched by the darkness that had consumed The Lurker? Or would she to be changed by the madness that had overtaken him?

The Lurker finally came to a halt at the edge of a clearing. He had done this before, lured his prey into the open, where there was no escape. But tonight, he wasn't sure who the hunter was anymore. Was it Alice closing in on him? Or was it him waiting for her to make her move?

The fog was so thick now he could barely see a few feet in front of him. It was in this silence that he could hear his thoughts screaming at him. What had he become?

He closed his eyes, trying to regain some semblance of control. He had always been in control, and always made the decisions. But now, his grip on reality was slipping. He couldn't keep running forever.

The voice in his head, the one that had been his constant companion, was louder now. It whispered things horrible things that made him question whether he was truly the one making the decisions or if something else was pulling the strings.

Alice moved cautiously through the woods, her eyes scanning the trees for any sign of movement. The fog seemed to swallow her, but she refused to let it disorient her. She had trained for moments like this. She knew that The Lurker's strategy was to wait her out, to force her to make a mistake.

But Alice was different. She had learned how to control the fear, how to embrace it. It was her only weapon in this silent war. Every step she took brought her closer to the truth, and she was determined to find it.

But deep down, Alice knew that this confrontation would change her. The Lurker had already changed, and she was beginning to fear what the chase was doing to her.

The Lurker heard her before he saw her. A faint rustle of leaves, he knew she was close. He was no longer interested in running. It was time to end it. He turned sharply, his eyes scanning the fog for any sign of movement. His heart pounded in his chest, his breath shallow.

He wasn't sure what he expected to find, but there she was, standing in the clearing, her silhouette outlined against the fog. Her eyes locked onto his, and for a moment, there was nothing but silence between them.

Alice took a step forward, her weapon lowered but ready. "It's over, Lurker," she said softly, her voice steady but tinged with something she couldn't quite identify.

The Lurker didn't move. His eyes were hollow, empty of the calculated fury they once held. There was nothing left in him but the remnants of the man he used to be.

"You don't understand," he whispered, almost to himself. "I've become something I can't undo."

Alice approached him slowly, her eyes never leaving his. "You don't have to do this. It doesn't have to be this way."

The Lurker looked at her, his face a mask of weariness. "I don't know how to stop anymore."

And for the first time, Alice saw the man behind the monster—the broken man who had lost his way.

The fog continued to thicken around them, the city now a distant memory. For a moment, there was no chase, no hunter, no prey, just two people lost in the dark, struggling to find their way back to the light.

But in that moment of silence, something shifted.

Alice and The Lurker standing in the clearing, both realizing the madness that had consumed them. As the fog rolls in and the tension builds, their paths are intertwined, leading to a confrontation neither of them could fully anticipate.

CHAPTER VIII

The Web Tightens

The air hung heavy with anticipation. The clearing, once quiet, now seemed to pulse with the quiet tension between Alice and The Lurker. Each had played their part in this deadly game of cat and mouse for far too long, and now they stood at an impasse. The city, with its towering buildings and buzzing life, felt like a distant memory. All that was left was the fog, the trees, and the two of them.

The Lurker's breath was slow and measured, though his mind raced. He had expected this moment to be one of triumph, but now, as he stared into Alice's eyes, all he felt was a hollow emptiness. She was the reason he had come this far. She was the one who had chased him to the brink, and now she was the one who might stop him. But could he allow that?

Alice's voice, soft yet firm interrupted his thoughts.

"You don't have to keep running," she said, her gaze unwavering. "I know you feel trapped, but you don't have to end this like this. You don't have to let the madness win."

For a brief moment, The Lurker considered her words. But they felt like a distant echo, like something from another life, a life he had long forgotten. The hunt had consumed him. The thrill, the rush of ending someone's life with precision—it had become part of him. How could he let go of that? How could he stop when everything he knew was bound to this twisted sense of justice he had created?

Alice took a step closer. Her weapon remained lowered, but the air between them was thick with unspoken tension. "I'm not your enemy," she said. "I'm just trying to stop you before you lose yourself completely."

The Lurker's fingers twitched at his side, a momentary lapse in his control. Was she right? Had he already lost himself? His mind was a warzone, and he was no longer sure of the rules of engagement.

"You don't understand," The Lurker finally spoke, his voice quieter now. "It's too late. This... this is who I am."

Alice shook her head slowly. "That's not who you are. That's who you've become. But there's still time to change."

The Lurker looked at her, his eyes clouded with doubt. "And if I can't? What happens then?"

There was a silence between them, a long, pregnant pause that seemed to stretch on forever. Alice didn't have an answer. She knew the truth, though. The Lurker had crossed a line. There was no returning from the path he had chosen. And yet, some part of her still held on to hope, hope that beneath the darkness, beneath the monster, there was a man who could still be saved.

Back in the city, things were spiraling out of control. The police had begun to close in on their investigation. They had been tracking The Lurker for months, but despite their best efforts, they were always one step behind. Alice had become their sole lead, but even she was unsure how much longer she could hold on.

In the investigation room, the team of officers, all seasoned veterans of the force, were beginning to lose their patience. The case had turned personal for many of them. The Lurker wasn't just a criminal; he was a symbol of everything they couldn't stop. His crimes had become more brazen, and more calculated, and they had reached a point where catching him seemed more like a dream than a reality.

Chief Rayburn paced back and forth, his mind heavy with the frustration of the case. "We're no closer than we were six months ago," he muttered, his voice hoarse. "How does a man like this slip through our fingers every time?"

One of the officers, Detective Morris, spoke up. "We're missing something. There's got to be a pattern, a clue we've overlooked. We're looking at this all wrong."

"Maybe," Chief Rayburn said, his voice sharp, "but we're running out of time. The Lurkers become a ghost, and Alice is our only lead. If she doesn't stop him, who will?"

Meanwhile, Alice continued to approach The Lurker. She could see the conflict in his eyes. She could see the rage and the pain fighting for dominance. He was on the edge, teetering between two worlds, the world he had created for himself, and the world she was trying to pull him back into. But he was no longer sure where he belonged.

"What happens if I can't stop?" The Lurker asked, his voice barely above a whisper.

"If you can't stop," Alice said softly, her heart heavy, "then you'll have to face the consequences."

But the consequences were already closing in on them.

As Alice spoke, a shadow shifted in the fog behind The Lurker. For a moment, neither of them noticed it. But the sound was unmistakable: a distant crack of a twig, the rustling of leaves, and then a soft breath in the night air. It was too late to turn back now.

Before Alice could react, The Lurker spun around, his instincts kicking in. His hand shot out, gripping Alice's wrist with surprising strength. She gasped, surprised by his sudden movement. "Stay back!" The Lurker hissed, his eyes wild.

But Alice wasn't afraid. She knew something he didn't: they weren't alone anymore.

Out of the mist, figures began to emerge. The Lurker's past had come back to haunt him. Old enemies, individuals he had left behind or discarded, were now closing in. The web that had tightened around him was no longer just Alice—it was a network of people who had been watching him, tracking him, and waiting for the right moment to strike. They knew his every move, his every weakness.

Alice's grip on her weapon tightened, but The Lurker wasn't worried about her. He was staring past her, his eyes locked on the approaching figures.

"Who are they?" Alice demanded, her voice steady despite the growing fear.

The Lurker didn't answer. He couldn't. He had already known that this day would come. He had known that the web he had woven was destined to collapse under its weight.

The figures closed in, revealing faces he recognized all too well. Rogue detectives, former partners, and criminals from his past. They had all come together, united by a single purpose, to bring The Lurker to his end. They were the ones who had once been part of his plan, the ones who had been discarded once they had outlived their usefulness.

But now, the tables had turned. The Lurker was no longer in control.

The fog felt thicker now, the weight of the situation settling over them like a suffocating blanket. Alice felt the tension between her and The Lurker grow, the weight of their past decisions pressing down on her. She didn't know who to trust anymore, but there was one thing she did know: the web had tightened, and there was no escaping it.

Alice and The Lurker face an unexpected alliance of enemies, each intent on bringing their twisted game to a close. The atmosphere is charged with fear, tension, and anticipation, setting the stage for an explosive confrontation.

CHAPTER IX

The Final Kill

The fog clung to the air like a suffocating shroud, hiding the figures that encircled them. The rustling of leaves, the crack of distant branches, and the sound of shallow breaths filled the oppressive silence between Alice and The Lurker. They were no longer alone in the clearing. Around them stood a group of figures, each shadowy form more dangerous than the last, their faces carved with the same hunger that had driven The Lurker to his madness.

Alice stood tense, her hand still clutching the handle of her weapon. She wasn't sure how many of them there were, but she knew one thing—they were all part of the same twisted game that The Lurker had once controlled. The irony wasn't lost on her. In trying to stop him, she had only played into his hand.

The Lurker's eyes flickered from one figure to the next, his breath shallow, his body tense. He knew them all. They were the ghosts of his past, the shadows he had created, each one a part of the web that had now closed in on him.

One of the figures—a man dressed in a long black coat—stepped forward. He was tall, his face obscured by a hood, but his presence radiated danger. His eyes gleamed with a cold, calculating malice. Jonas, The Lurker thought. An old partner in crime. A man who had once been indispensable to his plans, but who had been discarded when The Lurker no longer needed him.

Jonas' lips curled into a knowing smile. "You always were too careful," he said, his voice like a low growl. "But now, you're trapped."

The words hit The Lurker like a slap. Jonas wasn't just a former ally—he was a reminder of the person he had been before all this, a time when there had been some semblance of honor in the game. But now there was nothing left.

Alice stood her ground, her eyes shifting back and forth between The Lurker and the group closing in on them. She knew this was the moment. The moment when everything would either fall apart or come together. But in her gut, she felt the cold certainty that there would be no easy way out. The Lurker had made enemies of everyone—his past had come back to claim him.

Jonas stepped closer, the others following his lead, their eyes never leaving The Lurker. They moved with the quiet confidence of people who knew they had the upper hand.

"You've spent your whole life playing the game," Jonas continued, his smile never faltering. "But now it's over. You're the prey."

For a moment, the words seemed to hang in the air, suffocating all hope. The Lurker had always been the predator. He had hunted others without mercy, but now the roles had reversed. He was the hunted, and the surrounding darkness seemed to mock his every move.

Alice's voice cut through the tension. "This ends tonight," she said, her voice steady but fierce. "It's over, all of it. The killing, the games, the lies."

The Lurker turned to look at her, his expression unreadable. For a brief moment, he saw a flicker of something—a memory of a time when things hadn't been so complicated. But that was before the blood before the obsession had taken over. Now, all that remained was the darkness. The monster he had become.

"I've already told you, Alice," he said, his voice hollow. "This is who I am. And nothing can change that."

The group closed in, their weapons raised. The tension reached its breaking point. For Alice, everything seemed to move in slow motion—the heavy thud of her heartbeat, the shallow rasp of The Lurker's breathing, the chilling sound of metal scraping against metal.

Suddenly, a figure moved from the back of the group, and Alice's heart skipped a beat. It was Detective Morris—a man she had trusted. He was one of the last people she thought would be involved in this twisted scheme, but now, standing among the others, his face showed no remorse.

"Alice," Morris said, his voice soft but firm. "You don't understand. This is the only way to stop him. He can't be allowed to live."

Her grip on her weapon tightened, the weight of his betrayal crashing over her. Morris had always been part of the team. How could he have known about The Lurker's plans all this time? Had he been playing on both sides?

Before Alice could respond, The Lurker lunged. His movements were swift, a blur of calculated fury. In a split second, he tackled one man to the ground, his hand around the man's neck, squeezing with the strength of a man who had nothing left to lose.

The scene exploded into chaos. The Lurker fought with every ounce of rage and desperation he had left, but the odds were stacked against him.

Alice moved swiftly, taking cover behind a nearby tree. She couldn't let The Lurker win this time. She couldn't let him take anyone else's life. She had to stop him, no matter the cost.

The battle between predator and prey raged on, but it wasn't long before Alice realized the inevitable. She had underestimated just how far The Lurker had fallen. His fight was no longer about survival; it was about domination.

Every strike, every calculated movement, was a testament to how far he had descended into madness.

As the fight reached its peak, Alice finally made a decision. She couldn't save him. She couldn't fix what had been broken. There was only one way to end this.

With a steady hand, she raised her weapon.

The sound of a gunshot echoed through the foggy night.

The Lurker collapsed to the ground, his body hitting the earth with a finality that felt like the end of everything. Alice stood frozen, the weight of what she had done settling on her chest like a crushing burden. She had ended the game. She had killed the monster.

But what did it cost?

The fog seemed to shift, the world around her quieting as though the earth itself was mourning. Alice dropped to her knees beside The Lurker's body, her hands shaking, her breath ragged. She had done what she thought was necessary—but was it?

The city, now distant in the background, no longer seemed like the place it once was. Everything had changed, and Alice was left standing alone in the clearing, surrounded by the wreckage of a life that could never be fixed.

As she stood up, her gaze fell upon The Lurker's lifeless body. The hunter was dead. But the question remained, had justice been served? Or had they both been trapped in a game that would never end?

The night seemed to close in around her as she walked away, leaving behind the scene that would haunt her forever.

A haunting conclusion to The Lurker's twisted tale, leaving Alice to contemplate the true cost of her actions and whether justice had been achieved.

Epilogue: The Unseen Price

The city was eerily silent in the days that followed. People went about their lives, unaware of the horrors that had taken place in the shadows. The Lurker's reign of terror was over, but his legacy lingered like a dark stain on the city's soul.

Alice sat alone in her apartment, staring at the empty walls. The weight of everything that had happened pressed down on her chest, suffocating her. She had done what she believed was right, what she had to do to end the madness. But now, in the silence, she was left to wonder if there had been another way.

Could she have saved The Lurker from himself? Could she have stopped him without resorting to violence?

She didn't have the answers. All she had were the memories, the blood, the screams, the faces of those who had died because of his twisted games. And now, there was only an emptiness that gnawed at her insides.

In the weeks after The Lurker's death, the city began to rebuild. People spoke of him in hushed tones, as if speaking his name would bring the nightmare back. But Alice knew better. She knew that the monster was gone, but the darkness he had created could never be erased. It would haunt the city for years to come.

And then there was her.

Alice had become a symbol—a hero to some, a villain to others. The line between right and wrong had blurred, and she wasn't sure which side she stood on anymore. She had stopped The Lurker, but at what cost?

She walked the streets of the city late one night, her footsteps echoing in the emptiness. The fog rolled in, just like the night The Lurker had died. It was as if the city itself was still holding its breath, waiting for something or someone to emerge from the shadows.

As she walked, she glimpsed something out of the corner of her eye. A figure. Tall. Shadowy. For a moment, her heart skipped a beat. Was it him? Had The Lurker somehow survived?

But when she turned, the figure was gone.

It was then that Alice realized something profound. The Lurker's death hadn't solved anything. The evil that had festered in the city wasn't just one man—it was a system, a cycle of violence, corruption, and despair that one bullet couldn't destroy, one kill, or one person. The Lurker had been a symptom, not the cause.

As she stood there in the fog, Alice understood that she was now part of this ongoing fight—whether she wanted to be or not.

The Lurker's story was over, but hers was just beginning.

The sound of a phone ringing broke her thoughts. She pulled it from her pocket and glanced at the screen. It was a number she didn't recognize. Hesitating for a moment, she answered.

"Alice," a voice on the other end said. It was calm, composed, and eerily familiar.

"Alice, we know what you've done. But we're not done with you yet."

Her heart pounded.

The End?

This marks the conclusion of Lurker's Law. The story has come to an end, but the world remains fraught with shadows and unspoken truths. Alice's journey, like the city itself, continues forever intertwined with the dark past she cannot escape.

www.ingramcontent.com/pod-product-compliance
Lightning Source LLC
Chambersburg PA
CBHW022117150726

47990CB00003B/1387